D0041061

Millions of Americans remember Dick and Jane (and Sally and Spot too!). The little stories with their simple vocabulary words and warmly rendered illustrations were a hallmark of American education in the 1950s and 1960s.

But the first Dick and Jane stories actually appeared much earlier—in the Scott Foresman Elson Basic Reader Pre-Primer, copyright 1930. These books featured short, upbeat, and highly readable stories for children. The pages were filled with colorful characters and large, easy-to-read Century Schoolbook typeface. There were fun adventures around every corner of Dick and Jane's world.

Generations of American children learned to read with Dick and Jane, and many still cherish the memory of reading the simple stories on their own. Today, Pearson Scott Foresman remains committed to helping all children learn to read—and love to read. As part of Pearson Education, the world's largest educational publisher, Pearson Scott Foresman is honored to reissue these classic Dick and Jane stories, with Grosset & Dunlap, a division of Penguin Young Readers Group. Reading has always been at the heart of everything we do, and we sincerely hope that reading is an important part of your life too.

Dick and Jane

We Play Outside

Dick and Jane® is a registered trademark of Addison-Wesley Educational Publishers,
Inc. From BEFORE WE READ. Illustrations copyright © TK by Scott, Foresman and
Company. From WE READ MORE PICTURES. Illustrations copyright © 1951 by Scott,
Foresman and Company, copyright renewed 1979. From WE READ PICTURES.
Illustrations copyright © 1951 by Scott, Foresman and Company,
copyright renewed 1979. Text copyright © 2005 Pearson Education, Inc.

Published by Grosset & Dunlap, a division of Penguin Young
Readers Group, 345 Hudson Street, New York, New York 10014.
GROSSET & DUNLAP is a trademark of Penguin Group (USA) Inc.
Manufactured in China

ISBN 978-0-448-43616-6   11

Dick
and
Jane
We Play Outside

GROSSET & DUNLAP • NEW YORK

CONTENTS

Spot

Up, Spot, up.

Go, Spot, go.

Good, Spot, good.

Silly, silly Spot.

Puff

Come, Puff, come.

Come here, Puff.

Oh, Puff!

Run away, Puff.

Run.

Silly Spot

Come, Spot, come.

Come here, Spot.

Stay, Spot, stay.

Silly, silly Spot!

Sally Plays

Sally plays.

Sally plays in the sand.

Here comes Mother.

Look! Look!

Funny Puff

Look at Jane.

Look at Jane work.

Here comes Puff.

Look, Sally, look.

Look at what I can do.

Look at Puff.

Funny, funny Puff!

Funny Pam

Mother wants shoes.

Pam wants shoes.

Funny, funny Pam.

Funny Spot

Spot wants to eat.

Dick wants to eat.

Spot wants to eat more.

Funny, funny Spot.

Sally and Spot

Sally said, "No, Spot, no.
That is for me."

"That is not for you, Spot," Sally said.
"That is for me."

Run, Spot, run!

Run, Sally, run!

Father

"Look, look," said Father.

"A ball."

"What can you do?" said Dick.

"What can you do with the ball?"

Father said, "I can kick the ball."

"I can kick the ball with my foot,"
said Father.

Funny, funny Father.

Spot Wants to Play

Pam and Penny and Sally play.

Play, play, play.

Pam and Penny and Sally march.

March, march, march.

Spot wants to play, too.

Sing, Spot, sing.

Can Sally Play?

Sally wants to play.

Sally wants to play ball
with Father and Dick.

"Can I play?" said Sally.

"Can I play ball?"

See Sally play.

See Sally play ball.

Mother and Jane

Mother can sew.

Jane wants to sew.

Mother can sew.

Jane can sew.

Oh, no.

Silly, silly Jane.

Sally

Oh, no!

Look at that!

See Spot help.

Funny Spot!

Mike and Father

Mike and Father are in the park.

Mike buys popcorn.

Uh, oh! There goes the popcorn!

"Look, Father, look," said Mike.

"Look at the plane."

Mike said, "Look, Father, look!
Look at the birds.
Look at my popcorn."

Sally and Jane

Sally said, "What are you doing, Jane?
What are you doing with that bag?"

Jane said, "One, two, three!"

Sally did not jump.

Sally did not run away.

Spot jumped.

Spot ran away.

"Come, Spot, come," said Jane.

"Good Spot," said Sally.

Something Funny

Sally said, "Look, Jane.

Look at Dick.

Dick is funny."

"Look at me," said Sally.

"Look, Dick, look," said Sally.

"Look here.

You look funny. So funny!"

Sally and Dick

"Help, Sally, help!" said Dick.

Sally said, "Look, Dick, look.
Look at me."

"Look, Sally, look," said Dick.

"Look at me now."

Play

Sally and Dick play.

Sally and Dick play with the sand.

Dick wants to play with the water.

"I can help," said Sally.

"Oh, no," said Dick.

"That is too much.

That is too much water."

Play Ball

"Sit, Spot, sit," said Dick.

"I want to play ball."

Father said, "Go, Dick, go.
Play ball."

"No, Spot, no," said Dick.

"I want to play ball with Father."

"Go away, Spot!"

Sally Helps

Sally can help.

Sally can help Mother.

Oh, no!

Sally can help.

Sally can help Mother.

Dick and Mother

Dick can help.

Dick can help Jane.

Oh, no!

Who can help Dick?

Mother can help.

Mother can help Dick.

Sally and Father

Father can clean.

Father can clean the car.

Sally can clean.

Sally can clean the car.

Sally gets in the car.

Silly, silly Sally.

Sally and Grandmother

Sally can help.

Sally can help Grandmother.

"Help!" said Sally.

"Help me, Grandmother!"

Silly, silly Sally.

Mike

Father said, "Look, Mike.
Look what I have."

"Look, Mike.

Look what I can do."

Oh, no!

Mike can help Father.

That's better!

At the Farm

Dick is at the farm.

Dick is at the farm with Grandfather.

Dick can help.

Dick can help Grandfather at the farm.

The dog can help, too!

Mother Makes Something

"Look!" says Mother.

"Look at what I have.

I will make something for you."

"Look!" says Jane.

"Look at me."

Oh, no!

Dick and Father

"I will help," said Dick.

"I will help you with the pigs."

"Oh, no!" said Dick.

"Look! Look at the pig!" said Dick.

Dick said, "I will help you.
I will help you, Father!"

Go Home

It is time to go.

It is time to go home.

"Look!" says Grandmother.

"Here they come."

Now we can go home!

Penny

Penny said, "Did you see my shoe?"

Pam said, "No, Penny."

Mike said, "I can look.

I can look for your shoe.

Is your shoe in my bag?"

"No, no," said Penny.

"My shoe is not in your bag."

Penny said, "I can look.

I can look for my shoe.

I can look under the bed."

Pam said, "I can look.

I can look for your shoe.

Is it in the bed?"

"No, no," said Penny.

"My shoe is not in the bed.

My shoe is not under the bed."

Mike said, "I can look.

I can look for your shoe.

Is your shoe under here?"

Father said, "I can look.

I can look for your shoe.

Is your shoe in here?"

"Look!" said Penny.

"Look, look. Here is my shoe!"

Funny, funny Penny.

Funny Frog

Mike said, "Look what I can make.

I can make something fun.

I can make something fun for you to do."

"Look!" said Pam.

"I can hop. I can hop, hop, hop!"

Penny said, "Look! Look at me.
I can hop. I can hop, hop, hop!
I can pick up the stick, too."

"Look!" said Penny.

"The frog can hop, hop, too.

The frog can hop just like us!"

Funny, funny frog!

Grandfather

Good-bye, Grandmother.

We are going with Grandfather.

We are going on a walk with Grandfather.

What will we see?

"Look," said Grandfather.

"There is a school.

We will walk past the school."

"Look," said Penny.

"There is a man. The man is up high."

Grandfather said,

"The man is waving to us.

The man is waving to us as we walk past."

"I see a bus," said Penny.

Mike said, "I see a car."

"I see a truck," said Grandfather.

Pam said, "We can be a train."

"Wait for me!" Mike said.